Mary Richmond Baylies Allen

Reminiscences of the Baylies and Richmond Families

Mary Richmond Baylies Allen

Reminiscences of the Baylies and Richmond Families

Reprint of the original, first published in 1875.

1st Edition 2024 | ISBN: 978-3-38538-475-0

Verlag (Publisher): Outlook Verlag GmbH, Zeilweg 44, 60439 Frankfurt, Deutschland
Vertretungsberechtigt (Authorized to represent): E. Roepke, Zeilweg 44, 60439 Frankfurt, Deutschland
Druck (Print): Books on Demand GmbH, In de Tarpen 42, 22848 Norderstedt, Deutschland

Reminiscences

of the

Ba lies and Richmond

Families.

My Dear Children:

You have often asked me questions about our ancestry showing your interest and want of information on the subject. During the past few years I have for your exclusive benefit jotted down many things relating to both my father's and mother's families, the Baylieses and Richmonds. These recollections have grown so since I began them, that as I wish each of my children and grandchildren to possess a copy, it seems most convenient to commit them to print.

Allowance must be made for inaccuracies, as I have been compelled to trust largely to memory for facts, which I might once have gathered from dear ones now passed away. Hoping the perusal will afford you as much pleasure as I have received in transcribing, I commend it to your indulgence, attentive consideration and loving care.

M. R. A.

For full genealogical tables of the families included in this book and their collateral branches, see the "Family Record Book."

The Baylies Family.

THOMAS BAYLIES.

In the year 1687, there was born in old England to
Nicholas Baylies a son who was named Thomas. Of his
early surroundings, childhood and youth we know nothing.
but as he married at the early age of nineteen we must
conclude that he put away childish things and became a
man sooner than is common, certainly younger than his
descendants have done. As he was married after the
manner of Quakers, we suppose that one or both of the
parties belonged to that sect. In the genealogical record
of our family we have a copy of the form of this marriage
with the names of the witnesses, thirty-eight in number,
at the close. It is quite long and begins:

" *Whereas*, Thomas Baylies, son of Nicholas Baylies, of
the Parish of Alve Church, and the county of Worcester,
and Esther Sergeant, daughter of Thomas Sergeant, of
ffulford heath, in the Parish of Soly-Hull, in the county
of Warwick, Yeoman, having declared their intention
of taking each other in marriage before several public
meetings of the people called Quakers in Warwickshire,
according to the good order used amongst them, whose
proceedings therein, after a deliberate consideration
thereof, were approved of by the said meetings, they
appearing clear of all others and having consent of their
parents and relations therein concerned," etc., etc.

This document is dated Fifth day of the Fourth month,

commonly called June, in the year according to the English account one thousand seven hundred and six.

NICHOLAS BAYLIES,		THOMAS BAYLIES,
THOMAS SERGEANT,	} Parents' names.	ESTHER BAYLIES.
ELINOR SERGEANT,		

This is followed by the names of thirty-eight witnesses.

The Rev. Henry Baylies, my second cousin, when in England a few years since, visited the parish of Alve Church and examined the old church register, copying the records of the Baylies family in part, beginning in 1554, for three hundred years. After being engaged in the work for some time he was interrupted by the clerk, who informed him that he must pay half a crown for every name he copied. This led to some conversation, and the old man said that he would consult the rector. During his absence Mr. Baylies worked the faster. On the clerk's return he said that the law was inexorable, but that as he was an American he might take away the precious extracts without charge, for the love he bore that country, where he had some dear relatives.

Thomas (son of Nicholas) Baylies and Esther (Sergeant) Baylies, had eight children whose names were: Thomas, Ann, Hannah, Esther, Nicholas, Mary, Sally, and Helen. Ann married Richard Wycherly of London and settled there. They had three children.

Hannah married William Mould of London and settled there. They had a son and daughter.

Esther married a Capt. Holmes here in New England. They had three children, Elizabeth, Mary and Robert. Capt. Holmes was lost off Cohasset Rocks in 1743. He told his wife before sailing his last voyage, that if she

had a son, it was probable that he should never return, as in his family the father had not seen the son for many generations. This prophecy proved a true one.

Sally married Mathew Baker.

Helen married Peter Walker of Taunton. His farm was south of Westville, on the road to Mt. Hope Factory, and is still owned by his descendants. He died in 1762, and his will indicates that he had no children, as he bequeathed his farm to his nephew Peter. To his wife he left the negro Peggy, the two children and man Cambridge with £300. Also £3 yearly to Rev. John Lyon, for ten years, if he remained minister of St. Thomas church, Taunton.

Helen married for her second husband this Rev. John Lyon.

Mary married Col. Ezra Richmond my paternal grandfather, whose history I shall mention hereafter.

Thomas, the eldest son, was never married. He came to this country to visit his parents after their removal here, intending to return, but settled in Taunton and died July 21st, 1756, aged 41.

Of Nicholas 1 will write hereafter.

More than 30 years passed away after the marriage of our honored ancestors, Thomas and Esther Sergeant Baylies, before they came to this continent. The record reads: Thomas Baylies with his son Nicholas and daughter Esther, sailed from London, and arrived in Boston June 1737. He soon returned and the following year came over with his wife and daughters Mary and Helen. He settled in what was then called Attleborough Gore, now Cumberland, R. I. He was an "Iron Master" and came under contract with Richard Clarke & Co. of Bos-

8

ton, Mass. The original document containing the terms of their agreement written in London and dated Aug. 9th, 1738, is now in the possession of Rev. Henry Baylies and is a real "indenture," that is, the duplicate copies were written on one large sheet of paper and then indented, or separated from each other by being cut in and out, so corresponding with each other. For some years before coming to this country the family had lived in Colebrook Dale, Shropshire, Eng., where their son Nicholas was born. That is all I know of them, except their place of burial which I have seen. It is on the Taunton river and shielded by high bushes from the view of passers on the water. Some years since Frederick and I visited this graveyard and thought it the most dismal forsaken spot we had ever seen. It was overrun with briars and high tough grass, and received no new interments in many years. It was a Baylies burying ground for we saw few names except those of that family. From an old yellow scrap among my mother's papers, I copy the following inscription upon the gravestones of Thomas and Esther Baylies:

In memory of
ESTHER
Wife of Thomas Baylies
who died May ye 7, 1754
in ye 67 year of her age.

In memory of
MR. THOMAS BAYLIES
who died
March 5, 1756
aged about 69 years.

NICHOLAS BAYLIES.

Of the eight children of Thomas and Esther Baylies,
Nicholas the second son, was the progenitor of all of that
name in Taunton and Dighton. In fact, all in this country spelling their name in this way that I have ever seen
or heard of, traced back their family to this ancestor.
He was born May 19, 1719 in Colebrook Dale, England,
and came to this country with his father in June, 1737.
That he was as precocious as his father we infer from the
fact that he married at the same early age — nineteen
years. The only writing of his composition now remain-
ing is a love letter, which shows him to have been not
only susceptible to the tender passion but romantic in the
extreme. It is addressed to Miss Elizabeth Park of New-
ton, who afterwards became his wife. Would that we
knew where they met and how they became acquainted
with each other, for their homes were widely separated.

This letter, now in Mr. H. Baylies's possession, we have
been permitted to copy. It is written on a very large
sheet of paper in elegant handwriting, and reads thus:

UXBRIDGE FORGE, FRIDAY MORNING.

Dear Creature:

I hope by the powers divine, this little piece of writing
will find you in good health, and the same mind still af-
fected toward me, though now absent, as when I parted
with you, my dearest love. The reason of the Bearer's
coming down was I could no longer stay with patience till
I heard from you, and not knowing when Mr. Robinson
would come, for he is very fickle and almost distracted
with the thoughts of the happiness he intends to have in

matrimony. I throw myself at your lovely feet, with all
low submission, to crave one favor from my love. It is
not I alone but all of us implore your pity to us. Oh the
Gods! I hope will incline your heart to what I desire, if
not me I hope to your sister; that is you will favor us
with your company next week, for a horse will be down
Monday or Tuesday without fail, and myself — so if you
my love deny me this request you may as well sign my
death-warrant to him that loves you true. My only Life
and Happiness, it will be but a week sooner than our ap-
pointment which is nothing.

Oh the Gods themselves can't express the grief and
anguish, I endure in our separation, and if your heart was
as hard as the flinty rock, I can't but implore your mercy,
and yourself can't denie my desire. I shall be the un-
happiest of mortals if my fair one denies me an answer.
I desire and beg that my dear will write me all the news
she can. It is impossible for any earthly mortal to bear
the pain I feel in my Lovely Creature's absence. Oh you
must be hard and unpitiful if you don't take the way to
make me happy in your company. When your absence
will be my undoing and your presence the means of pre-
serving my life. I shall really think if you Denie me it
is your Brother that detains you. Oh if my only Love
has the passion for me as she said she had, or the Gods
deceived me if not you must have some love still for the
man who loves as Constant as I. If my dear is as uneasy
in the separation we endure you must have a mind to see
me once again. My mind is full of uneasiness for Fear
some one will Persuade you my Dearest love to be false
to the man whose Love is unspotted as the Turtle Dove.

Do pardon my impertinence for mistrusting my dear,
for it all proceeds from love as pure as Crystal Water.
The impatience I shall endure till the return of the mes-
senger to know that my dearest Life is the same as when
I left her, and if my starres blesses me with good news
from you, Oh The Gods, it will be impossible to express

the Transport of Joy I shall be in, and if unfavorable news it will be Death to my soul. Oh but I can't think that my dearest dear has so soon forgot me. May all the powers of Love protect you from harm is my heart's desire, and I beg a Thousand Pardons for this long and troublesome letter, which I hope your goodness will forgive.

You may certainly expect me Down and my love, favor me with a line or two. Pray give my service to all and my dearest Betsy, believe me to be, Dearest Creature, your constant though disconsolate lover.

NICHOLAS BAYLIES.

Your brother knows nothing but that the bearer had business yr. way.

In this manner my great-grandfather wooed his wife, the choice of his youth, with whom he lived in wedlock more than fifty years. Her wedding dress, a heavy, light blue brocade silk, with large figures of Chinese pagodas upon it, has to my great gratification lately come into my possession.

Her youngest son, Hodijah, left it to his daughter, Mrs. Dr. Wood of Dighton, from whose relatives (the Lincolns of Hingham) I received it. We are told that my great-grandfather was married in a peach-bloom silk coat with linen-cambric ruffles over his hands and bosom.

After their marriage they lived some years in Uxbridge, but upon the death of his brother Thomas, he removed to Dighton. Eight children were born to them.

Nicholas,	born	1739.	Thomas Sergeant,	born	1748.
Frederick,	"	1741.	Gustavus,	"	1752.
William,	"	1743.	A daughter,	"	1754.
Adolphus,	"	1745,	Hodijah	"	1756.

The only information we have regarding their domestic life I have received from my cousin, Mrs. Amelia (Baylies) Southgate. She writes:

"Some years ago, in a small Vermont village, I met an old lady over eighty years of age, who, finding my maiden name was Baylies, inquired if I were related to those of that name in Dighton. She said she lived there when a child, and her father was employed by a Mr. Baylies, who carried on iron works. As was the custom of the times, his workmen sat at the lower end of the table. One day some gentlemen from Boston were dining with him and asked Mr. Baylies with astonishment, why he had such men at his table. His reply was something like this: 'I prefer to have them at my table, for it is by these rough hands that I am able to live as I do.' The old lady told it with great unction, saying that she had often heard her father tell it. I felt rather proud of the old fellow and concluded that he was no snob at any rate."

I copy from the New England Geneological Register (Jan., 1866,) a brief notice of his life:

"Nicholas Baylies, with his father, Thomas Baylies, migrated to this country in the year 1737 from Colebrook Dale, Shropshire, England (to which place he had moved from Solihull, Warwickshire,) and settled in Uxbridge, Mass., where father and son engaged in the iron business, which they pursued in England.

"The rank, education and position of the family on their first appearance in this country were elevated. Esther Sergeant, wife of Thomas Baylies, was of a family belonging to the Society of Friends or Quakers in England. Nicholas Baylies represented the town of Uxbridge in the General Court as early as 1758. After his removal to Taunton he represented that town in the same body for the political years 1781-2, 1786-7. He was well known in

his day as one of the ablest politicians in Massachusetts, and though English born, was a most efficient supporter of America against British encroachments and through the revolutionary struggle.''

My great-grandparents lived to a good old age, and are buried by the side of their parents, Thomas and Esther Baylies.

A recent Taunton paper says:

About three and a half miles south of Taunton Green is one of the most ancient burying grounds in town, situated in a .retired spot on Taunton river. The genealogy of many of our present inhabitants may be traced on its monuments. It is singular that among its inscriptions there is but one indicative of the character of the deceased, and this is such as a bereaved husband might be allowed to give without being subject to a charge of flattery.

In Memory of

Mrs. Elizabeth Baylies

wife of
Mr. Nicholas Baylies
who died
February ye 8th
A. D. 1791, in ye 75th year of her age

The best of Wives
and the best of Mothers

THE CHILDREN OF NICHOLAS BAYLIES.

I desire here to give a very brief account of each of the children of Nicholas Baylies and his beloved wife Elizabeth, before writing of their fifth son, Thomas Sergeant Baylies, my grandfather.

Their mother's brief epitaph tells us she was " the best of Mothers" and if sons inherit of their mother more than of their father, we conclude that her children were of no ordinary stamp.

Nicholas, the oldest son, was born in Uxbridge, November 15, 1739.

In the family record book your will find the names of his four wives, and thirteen children, and also a long obituary notice taken from the New York "Spectator" June, 1831. From this we learn of his early conversion (joining the church when but ten years of age), and that his long life was spent in his Master's service. He was deacon of the church for forty-eight years, was a man of reading, reflection and prayer, and took a deep interest in all the benevolent enterprises of the day. He was an advocate of temperance and for more than sixty years did not taste of ardent spirits. He was a member of the convention which framed the constitution of this Commonwealth. He was a man of uncommon natural endowments, sound judgment, retentive memory, polite manners and kind and friendly disposition. He died in Uxbridge, Jan. 19, 1831, aged ninety-one years, where he had always lived.

Frederick, the second son of Nicholas and Elizabeth (Park) Baylies, was a farmer, and settled in what is now

called Southbridge, though his letters are dated "Stur-
bridge Farm."

Of his large family of thirteen children I was person-
ally acquainted with but one. This was his son Frederick,
who was in early life a schoolmaster, and afterwards became a missionary and teacher to the Indians in Rhode
Island, and in Marthas Vineyard, where he lived. He
was employed by the "Society for Propagating the Gospel
among the Indians of North America." He made an
annual visit to Boston and reported to its managers the
progress of his work. Prof. Kirkland of Harvard College
took a deep interest in his mission, always inviting
cousin Frederick to dine with him in Cambridge and it is
said invariably presented him with his last year's hat.
It is questionable whether similar gifts which Cardinal's
receive from His Holiness the Pope, give more satisfac-
tion than those which he bore to his island home. An
annual report of this society for 1819, thus speaks of Mr.
Baylies: "Mr. Frederick Baylies who has been employed
by this society for a long time as missionary and teacher
to the Indian schools at Nantucket, Marthas Vineyard,
and Charlestown, R. I., was employed again last year and
according to his statements the schools were kept sev-
enty-six weeks in all, by himself and others in his
employ. 'I have my trials,' he says, 'but am thankful to
God for the measure of prosperity which has accompanied
my labors, and that my prospects of usefulness are so
encouraging.'" There were many missionary stations
scattered throughout New England, and as the Indians
gradually decreased in numbers, the society sent a commissioner to visit the locations with the view of curtail-
ing the work. Mr. Baylies had heard of the movement

and was prepared to receive the visitor, there being no
public house on the island. When the packet arrived,
the guest was conducted to his humble dwelling with
Christian courtesy.

Mrs. B. was a good housewife and made the salary of
four hundred dollars a year go as far as any one could,
but that plainness of living was a necessity, we doubt
not. One of the viands set before the weary and fam-
ished gentlemen was a " Yankee Indian Pudding " in its
jelly, which was a specialty in her cooking. The "olive
plants," made ready for the occasion sat thickly around
the table. The neatness of the house, the setting sun
shining through the open windows, the summer foliage
of garden and fields, and the blue ocean all around, had a
pleasing influence on the feelings of the commissioner.
After tea, the conversation turned 'to the business in
hand, and the eldest daughter, a lovely girl with clear
complexion and gentle ways, took her seat beside her
father, an eager listener to the plans of the society as
they were unfolded. After listening for awhile she rose,
and standing by the speaker laid her hand upon his
shoulder and said, "Sir, are you going to dismiss my
father?" Whatever may have been his intentions, he
was so touched by her pleading tones and the influence
which surrounded them, that he replied, " No, no, my
child, I will not," and my cousin retained the position
while he lived. When Mr. Baylies made his annual
journey to Boston, he visited his relatives on the way and
often passed the night with us. No one was more wel-
come, and all enjoyed his cheerful and often humorous
conversation. He was a great walker, performing all his
journeys on foot. The distance between New Bedford

and Taunton was twenty-six miles and from there to Boston thirty-six miles more, which he accomplished with apparent ease. He died Sept. 30th, 1836.

William, the third son of Nicholas and Elizabeth (Park) Baylies, was born in 1743, and graduated at Harvard College in 1760. He settled in Dighton and was a member of the Provincial Congress in 1775. In 1784 while senator of the Commonwealth, Gen. Hancock appointed him Register of Probate for Bristol County and Judge of the Court of Common Pleas. He was a member of the convention that ratified the Federal Constitution. When he studied medicine I do not know, but he became an eminent physician, the most celebrated in the county in the latter part of his life. He died in 1826, aged 83 years. His two sons who lived to maturity were celebrated in the legal profession. William graduated at Harvard College in 1795 with the highest honors of his class. He became an eminent lawyer and had an extensive practice and the best business in Plymouth and Bristol counties for more than half a century. Of a large and magificent form, of great personal beauty and a most intelligent countenance he on great occasions spoke with admirable eloquence and power. He was never married and bequeathed his large fortune to Mrs. Nathaniel Morton, the daughter of his brother Francis. He died in 1865, aged 90 years.

Francis was distinguished in politics as well as in literary pursuits. He settled in Taunton and married the widow of David D. Deming of Troy, N. Y. He was for many years in the United States Congress and was also minister to Brazil for a short time. He published in 1828 a "History of Plymouth County," in two volumes

Betsey, the only daughter, married Samuel Crocker, Sr., of Taunton, of the firm of Crocker, Bush & Richmond. She was a valued friend of my mother's, their acquaintance commencing in girlhood, as their homes were near each other.

Hodijah, the youngest son of Nicholas and Elizabeth (Park) Baylies, born in 1756, graduated at Harvard College in 1777. His transition from college to the camp was immediate. He entered the Revolutionary army as Lieutenant, and his first service after recruiting was on the Hudson. When Gen. Lincoln was appointed to the command of the Southern Department he selected him as one of his aide-de-camps. When Gen. Lincoln capitulated Major Baylies became a prisoner of war, and as soon as his exchange was effected, he rejoined the army, and was called into the military family of Washington as one of his aides. After the surrender of Lord Cornwallis, Gen. Lincoln was appointed the first Secretary of War, and Major, then Lieutenant Colonel Baylies remained in Washington's family until the termination of the war, after which he spent some time at Mt. Vernon. In 1784 he returned to the North and married a daughter of Gen. Lincoln. After a short residence in Hingham, he removed to Taunton, where he owned iron works, and employed himself in their superintendence. When the present government went into operation under the Constitution he was appointed Collector of Customs for the port of Dighton and removed to that town. In 1810 he was appointed by Gen. Gore Judge of Probate for Bristol County. In 1834, at the age of seventy-eight, in the full vigor of his mental faculties, he resigned the office of Judge of Probate and retired from all public employment.

He was one of the handsomest men in the Revolutionary army. His bearing was martial, his deportment easy and graceful, and his manners polished and engaging. "Your son," said Robert Treat Paine to his mother, "has all the elegance of the British officers without any of their vices."

The vigor of his mind never failed, his perceptions were clear and acute. His conversation, marked with strong sense, abounding with anecdotes and interesting reminiscences of the Revolution, exhibited almost to the last days of his life the liveliness of youth without the garrulity of age. With the exception of Col. John Trumbull, he was believed to be the only surviving officer of the Revolutionary army. Though he rarely visited Taunton in his old age, yet I remember him and his old-fashioned costume—frilled shirt bosom, high boots with yellow tops and black tassels. I have been told that in his youth he was subject to hypochondria, was sure that he would be short lived, and changed his clothing with every change of the wind. At twenty, when greatly depressed, his brother, Dr. William Baylies, once said, "Hodijah, I'll insure you forty." He lived to be nearly ninety. He died in 1843, in the eighty-seventh year of his age.

THOMAS SERGEANT BAYLIES.

Thomas Sergeant Baylies, fifth son of Nicholas and Elizabeth (Park) Baylies, was my grandfather. He was born in 1748, and when twenty-one years of age married Bethiah Godfrey of Taunton and settled in Dighton, three miles from his brothers, William and Hodijah, in what was then called "Upper Four Corners." My grandparents, Thomas S. and Bethiah (Godfrey) Baylies, had eleven children.

Thomas,	born Sept. 15, 1770.	Henry,	born	Aug. 25, 1781.
John,	" May 9, 1772.	Charles,	"	July 1, 1783.
Polly,	" Apr. 23, 1774.	Clarissa,	"	July 6, 1785.
George,	" Mch. 31, 1776.	Alfred,	"	Sept. 16, 1787.
Horatio,	" Jan. 28, 1779.	Nicholas,	"	May 6, 1791.

John, born May 19, 1796.

I can say but very little of my maternal grandmother. When too late I regret that I did not seek the information I now desire so much, when I might have obtained it. I was seventeen years old when my father died, who no doubt would have gladly talked with me about his mother, but at that age the young are more apt to look forward than backward on the pathway of life. The following is the inscription upon her gravestone in the old Baylies burying ground.

In memory of

Mrs. Bethiah
wife of
Thomas Sergeant Baylies
Died October 30th, 1796
in the 47th year
of her age.

Step hither mortal, drop a tear,
Think on the dust that slumbers here,
And while with grief my grave you see,
Think on the glass that runs for thee.

Two or three years after the death of my grandmother, my grandfather married Miss Deborah Barnum, a daughter of the Rev. Caleb Barnum, the seventh minister of Taunton. His portrait and a sketch of his life can be found in Emery's "Ministry of Taunton." If his picture is accurate he must have been remarkably handsome, which could not be said of his daughters, three of whom I well remember, my grandmother, Mrs. Child and Mrs. Vickery.

This second marriage did not prove a happy one for the children. The new mother failed to make a harmonious family, and though kind and devoted to grandfather, endeavored to alienate him from his children. She always had her favorites among them, but was extremely fickle.

About once a year she would make peace with one or two of the sons, casting off her old favorites. This finally was often joked about and regularly expected by them. She had no children of her own, but many poor relatives depended upon her. They were not idle but worked in the family; still there was always much grumbling by the children on the subject.

To her extravagance and misuse of grandfather's means must be largely attributed the dispersion of his property.

For instance, she is reputed to be responsible for the appropriation and expenditure of a great portion of the inheritance of her (step) granddaughter Eliza Ann, which had been left in grandfather's care. On this orphan's marriage, suit was recovered by her husband, Mr. James Sproat against her guardian (grandfather) for the money thus lost. A part of the farm, already diminished by the unfortunate factory investment, was sold to meet this

demand, which amounted I believe to nearly twenty thousand dollars. As I knew little of grandfather's early life, I wrote for some information to his only surviving son (my uncle), Dr. Alfred Baylies of Taunton. I quote from his reply.

"To go back to my earliest recollection, my father then possessed a splendid farm under good cultivation, with stock to the amount of thirty head or more, four or five horses, fifty sheep, four or five hogs and plenty of poultry. This was on a farm of two hundred acres, and in the house the best wife and mother, a good daughter and nine unmanageable boys. I have no doubt that the farm came from my old grandfather Nicholas Baylies. This, however, is an inference I draw from the fact that each of the five sons had a good farm. My father was the conductor of a tanyard and was engaged in building vessels for the coasting trade and in farming.

"He sold to the factory company about half his farm and took a share in the same and lost it all and more. This brings me to the time and after the death of my mother and brother George, and the memorable marriage of my father to Miss Deborah Barnum, and then came misfortune of various kinds. Before I close let me explain the way in which Nicholas, John and myself came in possession of the old farm. Some ten year's before my father's death he told me if John and myself would raise him $1,000 he would give us a deed of the farm subject to a life lease. I told him we would do better. So I proposed to Nicholas that we three should raise $1,500, and this was accordingly done and deeds passed to that effect. After fifteen or twenty years we sold the remainder of this good farm of 70 acres for $2,500. And the estate of Thomas S. Baylies was insolvent. Not estate enough to pay funeral expenses. This looks strange, yes, passing

strange. Well, here I take leave of a very disagreeable subject with this reflection: what cannot be cured must be endured.

"When you come to Taunton I hope you will call on me, and I think I can convince you that all the Baylieses are not perfect, and that they mostly have better heads than hearts.

Yours truly,

ALFRED BAYLIES."

This epistle both in style and penmanship does credit to one in his eighty-fourth year. I remember my grandfather Baylies during the last twenty years of his life. He was a fine looking man, always wearing navy blue clothes with brass buttons. He was then in his old age and passed most of his time indoors in reading, though in pleasant weather he would drive to the Post Office in Taunton for the mail. He was not much of a talker and stammered, an infirmity which his son Alfred inherited. He always commanded great respect in his family. My recollections of the old homestead are very pleasant. I often dream of the dear old place as it was in the days of my childhood. Though still standing, its present diminished proportions bear but faint resemblance to that fine old mansion as it appeared in the early part of this century. Every room and closet in it is as familiar to me today as my own dwelling. The house was two stories high, standing on a slight eminence some distance from the road with a lawn in front. Though, there were outside doors on all sides the front door (painted green with a brass knocker) was at the side on the "lane" leading from the road. On each side were the square rooms, one the parlor and the other the family sitting room.

How well I remember the tall brass andirons in the old fashioned fireplace with the wire fender painted green in front, the deep window seats, the straight-backed chairs, three with cushions filled with feathers, the table with its complicated legs and carved woodwork; and in the corner the old London clock, which for aught I know was brought over by Thomas and his son Nicholas when they moved to this country. Back of these two rooms was a very long dining room the whole width of the house, with a large open fireplace on one side and an outside door facing the road.

Here sometimes twenty-five people were seated at dinner. The kitchen was in a two-story addition at the back of the house, but beyond the dining room and leading from it were two good sized rooms. One was grandfather's bedroom, a most comfortable apartment, where from its two windows could be seen the garden through the shrubbery near by, and the fields beyond. The other room was a pantry, then known as the "buttery," with a large lock closet within it. Here memory lingers. Here were stored the rewards for obedience. Though but little older than my darling grandchild Jojo now is (between four and five years), I well remember being led into the pantry and shown a row of blue and white bowls on the shelf and told to guess under which was something nice put away for me. If such trifling acts leave impressions so lasting, how carefully we should treat the little ones. Above these rooms were many chambers, fifteen rooms in all, well furnished, some of them handsomely. I cannot leave this homestead without speaking of the grounds that surrounded it, the shady orchard on the other side of the lane full of

valuable fruit trees. Here were golden sweetings, time-renowned greenings, seek-no-furthers, and winter russets, the tall pear trees bearing late fruit, the green pears with a red cheek, cherry trees where the birds chattered, notwithstanding the sleigh bells hung in the branches and often shaken. There were two gardens containing quince trees, red, white and black currants, gooseberries and all kinds of fruit. There was the old well-curb and long sweep, which finally gave way to the newly-invented windlass and crank; the broad flat door stone, where I sat many a time eating my bowl of apple and milk. Up the lane were great barns and cribs filled with plenty, and a great rock nearby covered with wild grape vines, where Cato the negro man would sleep in the sun.

The whole neighborhood was then alive with work people. There were two cotton mills situated half a mile from each other, known as the Baylies and Wheeler factories. In sight of the old place was quite a long lane leading to the Baylies factory lined with houses for the operatives, which was dignified by the name of "the city." Now all is changed, the houses are deserted, silence reigns at the mill where once was heard the hum of industry, and the city is desolation. The old home is kept in repair by its present owner, but it has been so modernized by the removal of the great chimney, alteration of the rooms, and tearing away of the outbuildings that it seems like another place. The beautiful orchard was leveled to the ground years ago and is now a green field, and what do you think met my gaze there the last time I saw it? A croquet ground! Shades of the departed! Had I seen Adam and Eve with some of their

sons and daughters engaged in this game I should not have been more surprised.

Children and grand-children at last left the old place, and Thomas Sergeant Baylies and his second wife Deborah Barnum, were left almost alone. In 1835 he paid the debt of nature and was laid to rest among his fathers in the Baylies burying place in Dighton. The wife of his youth, Bethiah Godfrey, rests beside him. Grandmother in her declining years lived in the old homestead, with only a niece to take care of her.

With the exception of the furnitue in her room, she disposed of all the rest, save the old clock which stood in its old place,—the empty sitting room,—alone, striking the hours so loud and clear.

"By day its voice was low and light,
But in the silent dead of night,
Distinct as a passing footstep's fall,
It echoed along the vacant hall,
Along the ceiling, along the floor,
And seemed to say at each chamber door—
Forever——never!
Never——forever!"

June 8, 1851, grandmother passed away, aged 85 years. Her relatives quickly and quietly took possession of all that they had not before obtained of the household effects, except the old clock, which still ticked on. Uncle John Baylies of New Bedford and I were both anxious to own it, so it was put up at auction and he obtained it, much to my regret.

27

CHILDREN OF THOMAS SERGEANT BAYLIES.

My father had nine brothers and one sister who lived to maturity. This sister, Polly, married William Andrews of Dighton, who went into business with my father. They removed to Frankfort, now Winterport, in what was then the district of Maine. She lived there until her death in 1857, when seventy-three years of age. She had two children, William and Mary. Their father built a ship for his son, naming it for his children "The William and Mary," and placed his son in command. After several voyages this young Captain William Andrews took the yellow fever at the West Indies. He became very sick on the voyage home, and one night in a fit of delirium came on deck and jumped overboard. This was such a terrible blow to his father that he allowed the ship ever to remain at the wharf, where it rotted to pieces.

The daughter Mary married Mr. Richmond Dean, who had also emigrated from Taunton. Some of their children, Mr. Bradford Dean and Mrs. Lathley Rich, you have met.

George, disliking country life, went to Boston, where he did a successful wholesale business on Long Wharf. He died at the early age of thirty-five years, leaving a handsome property.

His children were sent to his father's. The boys did not turn out well and died young. His only daughter. Eliza Ann, was a lovely girl and was very intimate with my sister Eliza. They were about the same age and she passed much of her time at our house before her marriage. She was handsome, agreeable, witty and quite an heiress,

which made her a favorite in society. She married Mr. James Sproat of Taunton, and died at the age of thirty-four years, leaving six children.

Horatio married Rhoda Pratt of Dighton, settled near his father and had eight children, of whom I know nothing except one son that lives on his father's place. His mother. who lives with him, is very aged and has been blind for many years.

Charles married Keziah Rounds and had six children; some of his daughters are now married and live near the old place, and his only son, Charles, resides in Taunton.

Alfred became a physician and was very eminent in his profession. He had an extensive practice and was much beloved by his patients. He married Rebecca D. Sproat of Taunton, by whom he had one son and three daughters. The son, Alfred, Jr., also became a physician, and married my cousin Jane, Uncle Charles Richmond's daughter, the third generation in which the Baylies and Richmond families have intermarried.

He died young leaving two sons, both of whom are now dead. Uncle Alfred married for a second wife Frances A. Williams and had two more daughters.

The youngest is named Esther Sergeant Baylies for her great grandmother who came from England and inherits a ring which has always descended to a namesake. It is gold, with a gold heart upon it and the initials *E. S. B.* Uncle Alfred lived to be eighty-seven years of age and died July 2, 1873.

Nicholas when a boy went to Boston and entered the store of George Baylies. When eighteen years of age he removed to Baltimore and became a clerk in the house of Nathan Tyson, flour and corn merchant. After remain-

ing in his employ for some years he went into partnership with a son of Mr. Tyson and continued in business until a few years before his death which occurred in Nov. 4, 1859, aged sixty-nine years.

He married Susan Stone of Baltimore and had thirteen children, seven of whom are still living. The sons are merchants in Baltimore.

John married Mary Shaw of Taunton and had nine children. For many years he lived in that place doing business as an auctioneer. He was noted for his wit and good humor. He afterward removed to New Bedford where he followed the same business. He died in 1863 aged 67 years. Several of his sons are in business in New Bedford.